*To Allyson. Best*

## Robin Darkmere

---

# THE CATHEDRAL CAT

Limited Special Edition. No. 14 of 25 Paperbacks

*Robin Darkmere*

Robin Darkmere was born in 1966 and has for the most part of his life been fascinated by the life and times of King Edward II. He spent twenty-eight years in the NHS in various clinical roles and served as an officer in Gloucestershire Special Constabulary before retiring. As well as writing, he enjoys photography and watercolour painting. He lives in Gloucestershire with his wife of thirty years and their four cats.

To all those I love, you know who you are.

Robin Darkmere

# THE CATHEDRAL CAT

AUSTIN MACAULEY PUBLISHERS™

LONDON · CAMBRIDGE · NEW YORK · SHARJAH

A CIP catalogue record for this title is available from the British Library.

ISBN 9781528986588 (Paperback)
ISBN 9781528986595 (ePub e-book)

www.austinmacauley.com

First Published (2020)
Austin Macauley Publishers Ltd
25 Canada Square
Canary Wharf
London
E14 5LQ

I would like to express my dear and heartfelt thanks to my wonderful friend, Kathryn Warner, who brought the life and times of King Edward II alive for me. Thanks also go to my wife, Kate, for her unending suggestions and interest in this project. My best friend, Sam, whose inspiration got me to write in the first place. My late father, who I was a constant scholarly disappointment to (I hope this book atones).

I would also like to thank everyone at Austin Macauley, especially Natalie Jones, Head of Editorial, for the wonderful opportunity to see my work in print.

Thanks also go to the Very Reverend Stephen Lake (Dean of Gloucester) Cathedral for his kind permission to use the cloister image on the cover; Karen Paynter, who works in the Cathedral shop; and, to Rebecca, the Cathedral Archivist, for her support and suggestions. Thanks also to Mesha Koczian, Emily Mongillo, Elke Kastner, Tracey Jaggers at Tewkesbury Abbey; Diana Haywood and Jan, who I spend Tuesday afternoons with in the Cathedral library, for their support and interest. Special thanks to everyone who reads this book and enjoys it. Blessed be!

# Chapter One

He had been lying in the sun of the cloister garden all afternoon and had been quite reluctant to move. The day had been long and hot and he had to muster all his strength and enthusiasm to so much as flick an ear occasionally to shoo away a fly.

Oswald, the cat of the Dean of Gloucester Cathedral, lived a good life. He could wander wherever he wanted, whenever he wanted all over the Cathedral and grounds and no one hindered him. He had not the slightest care in the whole world and it showed. He had been sleeping in the rose border on the North side of the cloister garden for some hours now. He liked the sun's touch on his stripy tabby fur as it permeated its way through to his skin. *It's a hard life being a Cathedral cat*, he thought to himself.

There were new scarlet blooms close to the ground on the roses near to where he was sleeping and a busy bee came seeking pollen to take back to its hive. The bee didn't bother Oswald. He barely cocked an ear as the bee buzzed about its business and then was gone as quickly as it had arrived.

The numbers of the visitors to the Cathedral were thinning out now, as the afternoon waned into the early evening. Soon it would be time for Evensong and also time for Oswald to seek his dinner from the Monk's Kitchen, as the Cathedral cafe was named, where Mrs Blake and her team, would always have a morsel of a treat for him. Sometimes it was left over tuna from the sandwich-making or it was pieces of hogget lamb left over from the making of the Pilgrim Pies, which were the speciality of the Monk's Kitchen. Whatever it would be, he was never disappointed.

The sun was lowering in the sky, its heat was fading and the Cathedral clock reached five p.m. As he rang out his sound, Great Peter, the huge medieval bell, counted out the hours one by one from his home near the top of the tower. Great Peter, was the oldest medieval bell still in regular use in England. Oswald had been up the tower stairs many times to visit him and stare in awe at Great Peter's size.

Great Peter had been cast on the grounds of the Cathedral before the reign of King Richard III. It had been a huge task to hoist him to his place in the tower and there he sat, for the next six hundred years and more. Around the top of Great Peter, there was an inscription cast into the metal, 'I was made for St. Peters Abbey', it read. Striking the hours of days and nights, Great Peter had been doing his job all these years.

*Oswald too had jobs to do at the Cathedral. It was his responsibility,* he thought, *to look attractive and inviting to the visitors. It was his actual job to ensure that the organ was properly in tune.* He had perfect pitch and could often be seen singing at the top of his voice in the choir during practices and services. The Dean had Oswald's red and white vestments specially made and he took his place next to a boy called Christopher, in the choir, Oswald looked very much the part dressed in his vestments. His favourites to sing were the Nunc Dimittis and the Magnificat. He particularly favoured the Magnificat. Anything with the words Magnificent and cat in the title simply had to be the best he always thought.

But now there was no time to waste. Mrs Blake would be closing the Monk's Kitchen and it was time for his first dinner. Oswald called it "first dinner" because he would receive another meal later on from his owner, The Dean. Oswald meandered his way through the cloisters and down the steps to the Monk's Kitchen. He knew he wasn't allowed in the actual kitchen itself and so he sat on the threshold of the door.

Mrs Blake was washing up the last of the day's dishes. She was so busy, she failed to notice Oswald sitting there patiently waiting for his treats. Oswald tried to gain her attention by wagging his tail to and fro. But Mrs Blake carried on washing dishes and singing to herself. Oswald listened carefully to the tune Mrs Blake was singing and then joined her in the chorus at the top of his voice.

"Bless me!" exclaimed Mrs Blake. "Is it that time already? Well, I had better get you your treat and quickly too, for Evensong will be starting shortly and we can't have you missing from the choir, can we?"

Oswald shook his head and Mrs Blake went to the fridge and fetched him his treat. She placed before him a small plate of tuna and Oswald began to eat, savouring every mouthful and showing his appreciation by purring loudly. Soon he was finished and licked the plate clean. "Good boy, Oswald!" cried Mrs Blake. "You ate it all. I bet you enjoyed that, eh? Now run off and get changed, it's time for Evensong."

Oswald turned and left Mrs Blake in the kitchen with her in full song. *Mmmm!* thought Oswald as he passed the stained glass windows of the cloister. *That tuna was lovely. Now all I need to do is find a quiet spot and have a good satisfactory wash. But there's no time, I can hear the organist striking up the first bars.*

After getting swiftly changed into his red and white vestments, Oswald leapt up into his place in the choir next to Christopher. Christopher was a small boy with blonde hair and was missing his two front teeth. Every time Christopher smiled at Oswald, Oswald would smile back and tried desperately not to laugh at the huge gap between Christopher's teeth that was so prominent.

Looking down the nave, Oswald could see that attendance to *this* Evensong, was particularly good. Most of the chairs were occupied and the Cathedral rang with the united sounds of organ and voices. Oh, how he loved the Cathedral and all its works.

After the Canon had said the last prayers, it was time for the choir to leave. The huge silver processional cross was carried by one of the vergers as he led the way down through the nave. Oswald was close behind and Christopher was close behind him, with his friend Henry by the side of him. As he passed each of the people sitting in the end chairs, Oswald could hear them say, either to him or to the person next to them that Oswald was a particularly good singer and a huge asset to the choir.

After entering the cloister and the great wooden door closed behind the last choir singers, it was time for all to go their separate ways. Oswald headed to the deanery in Millers Green, a square of ancient buildings not far from the Cathedral itself. The rest of the choir headed towards their dorms on the king's school grounds or to waiting cars and all the while the twelve bells in the tower sang out.

# Chapter 2

The deanery in Millers Green was a large house! Its front entrance was decorated with what looked like large stone vases with flowers in them on either side of the tall front gates. The house itself was from the Georgian period and was three stories high and was a very grand house indeed. Oswald made his way around the back to where his cat flap was situated in the lower portion of the back door.

As he approached the door of his flap, Oswald could smell dinner cooking. He sniffed the air deeply and savoured the aromas coming out from the house. *Could it be chicken?* he thought. *Or maybe it's roast pork. No, it's definitely chicken.* And with his mouth watering at the thought of his second dinner being roasted chicken, Oswald made his way inside.

Up the stairs was Oswald's favourite place, the main bedroom. In this room, he got to sleep in the middle of a large bed, in a large room. It was on this bed that he decided to sleep away the hour or so until dinner. He leapt up onto the bed, gave himself a brief wash and settled down to sleep.

The Dean was downstairs in his study writing letters and taking and making telephone calls. It was a busy life being the Dean of such a wonderful Cathedral and he took his job very seriously indeed. The door to his study was partly opened and as he saw Oswald pass and go up the stairs, he looked over the rim of his glasses and smiled to himself.

All the while the delicious aromas of roasted chicken and all the trimmings were coming from within the kitchen, where the Dean's housekeeper, Mrs Briggs, was cooking dinner. Mrs Briggs was a mature looking lady and had served the previous Dean with her housekeeping skills. Nothing ever out of place and everything was spotlessly clean. Almost every day the Dean would say to her, "I don't know what I would do without you, Mrs Briggs."

Mrs Briggs always wore her hair in a tight bun at the back of her head. Her clothes were usually always tweed and she never wore trousers. She considered it unladylike and always wore a skirt. She was rarely seen outside of the deanery unless she was shopping, picking flowers for the dining table, or receiving the post from the postman. She busied herself with her duties and was always reliable.

The clock in the hall of the deanery struck seven and with regimental preciseness, Mrs Briggs announced that dinner was ready on the table in the dining room.

Dinner was always at seven p.m. every day. Not a minute before and not a minute after. Mrs Briggs liked preciseness and stuck to it like a bear to a honey pot.

The Dean came out of his study and crossed the main hall to the dining room. He took his place at the head of the table with his back to the fireplace. All the food was under silver covers and one by one Mrs Briggs lifted them off to reveal perfectly cooked vegetables and a delicious roasted chicken. The Dean served Mrs Briggs first and she took her meal to eat in the kitchen. The Dean had many times reminded Mrs Briggs that he would enjoy her company at his table and that there was no need for her to eat in the kitchen. But Mrs Briggs didn't approve. She always replied that being the housekeeper, her place was in the kitchen.

And so the two of them ate their meals in separate places, just like every night. The Dean had taken to listening to music while he ate. It was a poor substitute for meaningful conversation, but it would have to suffice. As if by magic, Mrs Briggs appeared back in the dining room as soon as the Dean had finished eating. She did it every night and the Dean wondered how she always managed to come back into the room at precisely the right time. He never asked her though. He thought she might consider the enquiry impertinent.

There was always dessert at the deanery and Mrs Briggs had made a Spotted Dick with custard. A delicious marriage of light sponge and dried fruits steamed in a pudding basin.

After clearing away dinner, she brought the steaming pudding into the dining room on a plate and carried the jug of custard in the other hand.

"My, my, Mrs Briggs, that looks wonderful!" exclaimed the Dean. He could hardly control his excitement at the thought of hot sponge and dried fruits mingling with creamy hot custard.

"Aye, it were a favourite of ma mothers ye know?" replied Mrs Briggs in her broad Scottish accent. "I've made the custard with the cream left over from yesterday. I hope ye leek it."

"I am sure I will, Mrs Briggs. Let us have a cut and taste of this pudding, as that is where the proof lies, eh?" said the Dean.

"Aye!" replied Mrs Briggs. "The proof of the puddin' is in the eating, rich enough," she replied.

It was truly a delicious pudding and both the Dean and Mrs Briggs enjoyed it immensely. Mrs Briggs always refused any assistance with clearing the table and so the Dean returned to his study to make a call to Bishop Harriet, who lived in the Bishop's Palace down the road. He could walk down to see her, but he didn't like to arrive unexpected and as he lifted the telephone receiver and began to dial, he saw out of the corner of his eye, Oswald making his way down the stairs to the kitchen.

Oswald was allowed in the deanery kitchen as long as he kept all four of his paws on the floor and not on the chairs or the worktops. Mrs Briggs had prepared him a dinner of cooked chicken and gravy. "Poor wee thang. Ye must be starvin' havin' gane all this tame since breakfast, so 'ave prepared ye an extra-large portion. But nae be tellin' the Dean." Mrs Briggs placed the plate on the floor chuckling to herself and then went about her duties as Oswald tucked in. Mrs Briggs enjoyed Oswald's company and liked, even more, to spoil him with larger portions that he really shouldn't have. But the Dean didn't mind and neither did Oswald, so what did it matter?

After every juicy mouthful had gone, Mrs Briggs picked up the plate to wash it and placed it on the draining board of the kitchen sink. She looked down at Oswald, who was expecting his dessert. "My, my!" exclaimed Mrs Briggs. "Dessert as well? Och well, it cannae do nae harm." As she bent down with another plate, Oswald could see it was a dish of cream custard and as he lapped it up, Mrs Briggs looked on, smiling.

Later that evening, the clinking and clattering from the kitchen had ceased, the telephone in the Dean's study had stopped ringing and the deanery was silent, apart from the occasional spit and spark from the fire in the drawing-room. The Dean was sat in his usual chair by the fire reading the newspaper and sipping a warming glass of sherry. Oswald was in his usual chair on the opposite side of the fireplace, curled up asleep and purring. He didn't even stir when Mrs Briggs popped her head round the door to announce that she was about to retire for the night. "I'll be awa' tae ma bed the now, Dean."

The Dean looked up and smiled and said "Good night, Mrs Briggs. Sleep well."

"Aye!" replied Mrs Briggs. "I will."

The Dean dropped his eyes back to his paper and resumed reading as Mrs Briggs could be heard making her way up the stairs to her room and her well-earned bed. The clock on the mantelpiece chimed ten o'clock. Its chimes were steady and tuneful and were always a sound of comfort to the Dean. Just then, a few minutes behind, the clock in the hall chimed ten and its sound echoed through the deanery. No matter where he was in the house, the Dean always knew what time it was, whether he could see a clock or not, as they could be heard in every room from the cellar to the attic.

Did it disturb his sleep? No, not at all. Both the Dean and Mrs Briggs were quite used to it by now and so was Oswald to that fact. Not that anything could actually disturb Oswald from his sleep after such a big meal. But little known to Oswald, tonight was going to be different.

# Chapter 3

The night had fallen softly with the calm of falling leaves. As she rose in the sky, the waxing Harvest Moon cast silvery shadows on the ground making intertwining dark patterns on the grass through the bare twigs and scant leaves of the trees. The sky was like a deep dark blue blanket studded with stars that twinkled like sequins. Up in the Cathedral Tower, the bells chimed away the hours until daybreak and there was a wintry feel to the breeze that promised rain before dawn as it swept across the Cathedral gardens.

In the deanery, Oswald was snuggled into his favourite chair in the drawing-room and was dreaming of the roast chicken dinner he had earlier that evening. The fire in the grate was now nothing but embers glowing against the dark of the room but still, it kept him warm.

Great Peter, dolefully chimed the hour of one o'clock and Oswald was awakened. This was unusual as Oswald was never disturbed by the bells in the tower. He raised himself and stretched and for a minute looked all around himself at the drawing-room. With his keen eyesight in the dark, Oswald was able to see everything and everything was as it should be. So he snuggled back down after turning once or twice in a circle and began to wash himself. He began with his front left paw, as he always did. Not that it needed washing, that was just the place he always started to wash.

Still, something wasn't quite right about the night and Oswald decided to investigate. He got out of his lovely warm chair and jumped up onto the window sill and peered out into the night. Outside of the window panes, Miller's Place was dark and silent. Oswald made his way to his flap at the back of the house and without further thought, he made his way towards the Cathedral. He went past the arches and pillars of some ancient abbey buildings, that were long forgotten to the mists of time and he made his way across the Cathedral's North lawn.

Despite all the doors and windows being secured, Oswald knew a way into the Cathedral that was just big enough for him to get through. It was a small hole in a grating at the front of the Cathedral near the Lady Chapel. Once he arrived at his secret entrance, he looked over his shoulder to make sure he wasn't being followed. As he made his way in, Oswald's shoulders rubbed against the iron bars of the grating a little more than usual and he decided then and there that maybe one dinner each night would suit him better.

The silence inside the Cathedral was deep. Not a sound could be heard in the dark from the Tribune Gallery on the first floor, down to the crypt in the basement. The air was still and heavy with over a thousand years' worth of history giving substance to it. Oswald made his way down through the Cathedral towards the South Transept using his keen feline eyes in the dark. Looking through the archway into the main choir, Oswald could see a strange bluish glow. It was moving about and Oswald was curious to see what it was.

It is said that curiosity killed the cat, but Oswald had no fear of old sayings. He simply had to see what the bluish glow was, so he made his way steadily towards it. Creeping low on his belly, across the choir, Oswald looked quite insignificant below the main altar and the huge Great East Window above it. He crept further and further towards the glow until he was able to peer gingerly round the corner of an archway.

All was as it should be. The glow was nowhere to be seen. *How odd*, thought Oswald, *where could it have gone?* He crept on his belly ever so slowly round the stone corner of the archway, keeping low, moving silently inch by inch. In front of him was a single stone step and Oswald stretched his entire body against the riser, so he couldn't be seen from the direction the blue glow had been.

Then, ever so slowly, Oswald looked up over the riser of the stone stair. First, his ears appeared, looking almost like shark fins cutting the surface of the water. Then the top of his head appeared with its stripes and then two sharp green eyes with massive pupils and a bright pink nose appeared. What did he see? Nothing! Absolutely nothing, well, nothing out of the ordinary anyway. From what he could remember of the curious glow's position, it should have been where the tomb of King Edward II is. *Perhaps it was the king's ghost,* thought Oswald, joking to himself.

Oswald didn't believe in ghosts, or at least he believed they couldn't harm him. It was the living he had to be more careful of. How many times he had narrowly escaped with a chicken leg from the king's school's Headmaster's kitchen window without being soaked with a jug of water, he couldn't remember.

All was silent and all was still and nothing was out of place. Oswald decided to investigate further and left his safe haven below the riser of the stone step and slowly crept his way towards where he thought he had seen the blue glow. Step by step, he crept towards the tomb. He looked up at its beautiful decoration and the effigy of the king himself lying on the top of the main section, looking like he was serenely asleep. He edged closer still and began sniffing the air. Nothing was there that should not have been and after Oswald had made his way around the entire tomb, he was satisfied that all was well.

He sat in front of the king's tomb and washed the end of his long stripy tail. He had to almost fold himself in half to do this and after a few licks, he decided to go back to his chair at the deanery. Giving himself one or two more licks, Oswald was about to turn around and make his way home when a voice spoke out, "Well, what have we here? A little stripy cat!"

Ahhhhhhhhhhhhhhhhhhhhh! Oswald leapt high into the air with fright at the sound of the voice behind him and ran back through the archway into the main choir, through the South Transept and out through his secret entrance and didn't stop running until he was back in his chair in front of the fire. His heart was pounding like a steam train and he panted to catch his breath. He had cannonballed his way through the flap in the back door and had nearly knocked it off its hinges.

Some of his fur still stood on end as the clock in the hall of the deanery chimed half-past two. Oswald wasn't going to be able to sleep another wink that night. *What could that blue glow possibly have been?* thought Oswald. *And where on earth did that person come from that nearly scared all nine lives out of me at once?*

All through the rest of the dark hours, Oswald pondered these questions and the more he pondered them, the more confused he became. He had been alone in the Cathedral, surely. Maybe it had been one of the vergers? But that was impossible, as he knew all the vergers and what their voices sounded like and the voice he had heard was not one of theirs. *A thief perhaps?* he thought. *Yes, that was it, someone had been hiding in the Cathedral since lock up after Evensong and lie in wait to steal things. But why stay in there until the small hours of the morning?*

*Drat it,* thought Oswald! Try as he might sleep eluded him. He would have to wait until morning to go and have another look at King Edward's tomb and try to make head or tail of this whole thing and until then, there was nothing he could do.

He turned a few circles in his chair and wrapped his tail around himself, closed his eyes and catnapped until the dawn rose over the Cathedral in the grey eastern sky.

# Chapter 4

Breakfast was a completely different ritual at the deanery than dinner was. It was a much more relaxed affair. Mrs Briggs would set everything out in the breakfast room which was at the front of the deanery. Its window overlooked Miller's Court and was usually flooded with sunlight. But today, the skies were grey and the rain was falling in a very melancholic way. The breakfast room was a pale lemon colour and all the skirting boards and doors were a dazzling white. The sideboard at the back of the room was a deep dark oak and was set out with fresh fruit, cereals, fruit juices, and tea and coffee. In the kitchen, Mrs Briggs would have a cauldron of porridge on the stove and on the hot plate in the breakfast room would be the cooked breakfast items.

Sausages were a particular favourite of Oswald and he would sit patiently by the table leg waiting for the Dean to 'accidentally' drop a sausage down to him. This was a practice that Mrs Briggs did not approve of and would often remark, "What is Oswald eating? I hope ye have nae been feedin' him 'neath the table, Dean. Sausage makes greasy marks on the rug."

"Perish the thought, Mrs Briggs," would be the Dean's usual reply, but they both knew the truth. Once he had finished eating, Oswald changed into his vestments and made his way to the main quire for Matins. The duties of the Cathedral Cat were many and Oswald attended to every one of them.

The clock in the hall, faithful as ever, chimed nine and with breakfast done, the Dean made his way to his study to begin the day's work. He had to find some notes he had made for a meeting with Bishop Harriet later that morning and so he occupied himself looking for them.

Outside, the rain was making everything wet and dull and Oswald made his usual way across to the cloisters, as the door would be unlocked for visitors, as quickly as he could. All around him the slates on the roofs of the buildings were shiny and wet. As he trotted, he could feel drops of icy rain dripping from his spiky fur and it wasn't pleasant to him.

Once he was under the canopy of the cloister entrance, Oswald gave himself a good shake, from the top of his head to the tip of his tail. The wall of the cloister entrance was splattered with tiny droplets of water and it made the sandstone a little darker in colour. Just across the pathway from where he was sitting, was the herb garden. It had been there for centuries and even now, herbs were being grown in the soil there. Oswald sniffed the damp air and could smell Parsley, Rosemary and all kinds of other herbs.

Oswald had spent many a day in the herb garden, sleeping the sunny hours away until the next meal. Centuries ago these herbs would have been used by the monks of the abbey for cooking and healing. Now, they were mainly grown for decoration and as a spectacle for the visitors.

Oswald could hear footsteps echoing in the cloister and he rounded the corner to see to whom they belonged. It was Mrs Blake, on her way to the Monk's Kitchen to begin making sandwiches and soup to be served to the customers visiting the Cathedral. He was about to follow her knowing full well he would get a treat of something. But two things stopped him in his tracks. First was the thought of the blue glow he had seen the night before and the voice that had scared him nearly out of eight of his nine lives and secondly the fact that he had to squeeze himself through his secret entrance.

Instead of following Mrs Blake to the kitchen, he made his way through the cloister and towards the big red doors at the top of a small stairway that opened up near the North Transept. From there, it was only a short walk up the stairs and through the arch to where he had been the previous night. He climbed the stairs, up through the small archway and there he was in front of King Edward II tomb. The spotlights in the ceiling were glowing especially bright inside because it was so dim and dismal outside and they caused the dark coloured Purbeck marble at the base of the tomb to seem even richer in colour than usual.

In fact, the whole decoration of the tomb from the very bottom to the ornate pillars that looked like spires on a church at the top seemed to glow in the light of the spot lamps. *That doesn't explain the blue glow I saw last night,* thought Oswald, and he decided to make his way around the back of the tomb for a closer look. Nothing appeared out of the ordinary and just as Oswald appeared back in front of the tomb, he was addressed by a kindly voice.

"Hello, Oswald. How are you today my fine fellow?" It was one of the lay preachers whose task it was to climb the stairs of the pulpit in the main choir and say the hourly prayer over the Cathedral's Tannoy. The visitors to the Cathedral were always asked to stand or sit in silence and join the preacher in prayer. Most did and Oswald would usually stop what it was he was doing, in mutual respect.

Oswald rubbed around the bottom of the lay preacher's black robes and purred loudly.

"What are you going to get up to today, eh?" asked the preacher as he looked down at Oswald rubbing around and leaving hair on his black robes. "Now Oswald, that's enough of it. I need to look my best for the hourly prayer. I will see you later at Evensong."

Oswald stopped rubbing and the preacher made his way to the pulpit with a huge smile on his face. All the people in the Cathedral liked having Oswald around, he was pleasant company and he liked the attention he got in return equally as much.

At this hour of the day, there were never many visitors and it was usually quiet. Oswald was sat looking at the king's tomb in quiet contemplation. He let his mind drift to wherever it wanted to roam and roam it did. So much so that he was unaware of a slight tugging at the tip of his tail. He looked round and saw his old friend Gideon the mouse.

Gideon was dressed in his black vestments and had the white-collar of the holy office around his neck. Gideon had been at the Cathedral for years and was, to all intents and purposes, the Vicar for all the mice that lived there. He held regular services up in the eaves of the roof of the South Transept and they were always very well attended by all the mice.

"Hello, Oswald," greeted Gideon.

"Hello, Gideon. Fancy seeing you here. You're usually in the eaves of the South

Transept roof. What brings you down here?"

"Mrs Blake throws out all the breadcrumbs from the kitchen, she leaves me a small plate of them and I go to have my breakfast. Sometimes I'm lucky and the crumbs have butter on them or even better, jam. You look rather glum there, something up?"

Oswald wasn't sure he wanted to share the previous night's happenings with Gideon. He couldn't explain what it was he saw nor who it was who had spoken and his little Vicar friend probably wouldn't believe him anyway.

"I'm okay Gideon," replied Oswald.

"If you were to say the great East Window had lost all its colours in the rain, I would believe that, but not what you just said. What's up, old friend? You look like you have seen a ghost!"

At hearing this, Oswald turned and looked at Gideon with surprise. Maybe that was it, maybe it *had* been a ghost he had seen.

He had never been any good at hiding his feelings and now that Gideon had sensed something was in fact, bothering him, he felt obliged to share his story. Oswald walked round the back of the tomb and beckoned Gideon to follow him. Once they were both safely ensconced, Oswald told Gideon everything about what happened the previous night. While he did so, Gideon sat on his hind legs and looked up at Oswald, over the round wire rim of his glasses, listening with keen interest. Once he had imparted all, Gideon sat and smiled to himself.

"Oswald, my dear friend," said Gideon. "It was indeed a ghost you saw." His voice was calm and steady and very matter of fact. Oswald knew by the tone of Gideon's voice that he wasn't joking.

"A ghost!" exclaimed Oswald. "But who's ghost is it and how come I have never seen it before?" There was a slight edge of disbelief in Oswald's voice and Gideon detected it.

"There are many things in this great old building that go unnoticed," said Gideon, looking about him. "Hauntings among the rest. It is usually about this time of year when the ghost of King Edward II walks abroad in the Cathedral."

Oswald was amazed and his expression showed it. "Why now Gideon?" he asked, perplexed. Oswald had wandered through the Cathedral on many a night and never seen this ghost of the king, ever.

"Well," said Gideon. "It is said that back in September 1327, King Edward II, was murdered. He apparently died a horrible death some say and for as long as I can remember, his ghost has risen every September since his burial in this tomb here," Gideon pointed to where the edge of the marble met the tiles of the floor.

"What does he want?" enquired Oswald.

Gideon looked up at his friend and smiled. "What makes you think he wants anything?"

"I don't know," Oswald said wistfully. "Seems odd that he should want to walk the

Cathedral after dark and not want anything."

"Well…" mused Gideon. "Whatever the answer is, maybe you are right and maybe you are not."

Gideon bid Oswald a good morning and went to the verger's office to ask for more candles for the candle sticks on the small altar that he had in the eaves of the South transept. Soon it would be time for Prime the main service of the day and all the mice in the Cathedral would be gathering for it.

Oswald made his way to his favourite corner of the Chapter House, instead of the cloister garden, as it was still raining. He decided to sleep on a cushion until it was time for

Evensong. There were big iron gates to the entrance of the Chapter House and Oswald could squeeze between the railings with ease. There was little if no sound at all and Oswald was soon asleep.

His sleep was restless! He was dreaming of King Edward II's ghost and how it had frightened him into running out of the Cathedral that night as if he had his tail burned off. So there he lay in the Chapter House, all comfy and warm. Some of the visitors to the Cathedral saw him through the iron gates and pointed him out to other visitors, but for the main part, he was left undisturbed.

Oswald liked the Chapter House very much, for it was in this very room in the year 1088 that King William the first commissioned the Domesday Book. Oswald loved the history of the Cathedral and loved being a part of its daily life.

Great Peter began to toll for Evensong and Oswald awakened. He stood up and had a huge stretch. His body elongated to almost twice his normal length and he let out a very satisfactory yawn. He then went to get changed into his vestments and then made his way on up to his place in the choir, next to Christopher.

Evensong was soon over and Oswald was on his way to the deanery for dinner. He made his usual route to his flap and gave a large sniff to see what Mrs Briggs was cooking. To his very sensitive nostrils came the aroma of steak and kidney pudding, with mashed potatoes, carrots and peas. He didn't care much for the carrots and peas, nor for the mashed potatoes for that matter, but the steak and kidney pudding was high on his list of expectations.

Oswald was halfway along the long hallway that divided the deanery in two, when the large front door in front of him opened and the Dean appeared all sodden and wet. The Dean turned his back on Oswald and gave his umbrella a good shake before allowing it to enter the house. Mrs Briggs wouldn't appreciate a puddle on the nicely polished quarry tiles that were on the floor. The Dean removed his coat and placed the umbrella into its stand by the door. He looked down at Oswald and said, "Hello, Oswald old chap. How are you?"

Oswald looked up at the Dean and chirruped an answer. The Dean laughed and said, "I bet you haven't ventured outside in that rain today, have you? Can't say I blame you."

"Is that you, Dean?" came Mrs Briggs' voice calling from the kitchen.

"Yes, Mrs Briggs, it is I," the Dean replied. Just for his own amusement, he had always wanted to make a witty reply but always thought better of it in case his brevity offended his devoted housekeeper.

"Dinner will be on the table in twenty minutes, Dean," called Mrs Briggs.

Without having to look at his watch, the Dean knew the time was twenty minutes to seven and he made his way upstairs to ready himself to eat.

He had put on a pair of black corduroy trousers, a checked shirt and a lovely Fair Isle jumper that Mrs Briggs had knitted and given to him as a Christmas present. He felt that this would keep him snug and warm, as the weather outside was still cold and miserable. He made his way to the dining room and as usual, sat in the chair with his back to the fireplace.

Oswald, meanwhile, was making his way to the kitchen, where he would be served his dinner. He sat in his usual corner of the kitchen and patiently waited for Mrs Briggs to oblige him.

The Dean was served his dinner and Mrs Briggs began to make her way to the kitchen table. As she turned towards the door the Dean spoke up. "Mrs Briggs!" he began. "I should very much appreciate your company at dinner this evening. Please, take a seat and join me."

As dumbfounded as she was, Mrs Briggs turned and gave her answer. "Are ye sure Dean? I dinnae mind the kitchen."

"I know, Mrs Briggs, but your company would be very welcome to me."

Mrs Briggs took a seat opposite the Dean at the other end of the table. She wasn't used to the idea of eating in company and she wondered as to what the Dean's motive might be.

Mrs Briggs had need not worry. The Dean made all kinds of pleasant conversations with her and she began to relax and enjoy the company and the surroundings. The fire cracked and spat in the grate and the meal was enjoyed by the pair of them. During their conversation, the Dean remarked that a concert was to be played in the main choir on Saturday evening and he asked if Mrs Briggs enjoyed the music of Ralph Vaughan Williams.

"Aye, Dean. I do," she replied and told an anecdote of when she was a wee girl back home in Glasgow, her mother took her to such a concert at the Pots and Pans theatre on Trongate.

"Pots and Pans?" queried the Dean. "That's a very odd name for a music hall, Mrs

Briggs!" and he began to chuckle.

"Well, Dean, ye see it was actually called the Britannia Panopticon, but we folk called it the "pots and pans,"" and she too began to laugh, as she remembered how the manager of the Music Hall disliked the nickname the customers gave it.

"I should very much like you to accompany me to the concert, Mrs Briggs," said the Dean, coyly.

"Michty me, Dean!" Mrs Briggs replied in surprise. "I wasnae expecting that. I couldn't go, there's far too much to do. I mean, how would dinner get cooked?"

"Well," returned the Dean, "I was rather thinking of taking you to dinner first if that would be agreeable to yourself, Mrs Briggs." He wasn't sure whether it was the glow of the fire or the post dinner sherry in her glass that was causing the ruddiness in her cheeks, but Mrs Briggs appeared to be blushing.

"Oh do say you will accompany me to dinner and to the concert, Mrs Briggs. It would be a most agreeable evening."

With another sip of her sherry, for moral support, Mrs Briggs replied that she would accompany the Dean to dinner and to the concert on Saturday.

Mrs Briggs cleared the dinner table as the Dean returned to his study. Oswald, as usual, was awaiting his dinner and was sat by his bowl in the kitchen. Mrs Briggs bent over and picked up the empty bowl and returned it to Oswald, full of meat and gravy, which he enjoyed thoroughly. As Mrs Briggs washed up, Oswald enjoyed a saucer full of cream that had accompanied the apple pie they had for dessert and Oswald enjoyed that even more than the bowl of meat.

The clocks in the deanery all chimed ten and Mrs Briggs put her head around the study door to thank the Dean for his company that evening and also for his kind invitation to Saturday's concert.

"You are most welcome, Mrs Briggs; I am looking forward to it already."

"As I am, Dean," she replied. She stood in the doorway smiling and wasn't really sure as to what her next sentence or move should be. It seemed to her that she had been smiling at the Dean in the doorway for an age and she couldn't draw herself away.

All the Dean could do was to sit in his desk chair and smile back at her. It had been a most lovely evening and he had no desire for it to end just yet. As he looked into her eyes, he could see that the woman who stood before him, was not as old as she dressed or acted. He could see that she was much of an age with himself. He could see that losing her husband and becoming a widow, had aged her prematurely and this was the reason she dressed the way she did.

The silence between them was now an agony. He searched for words to break it but none would come. He felt the inclination to rise from his chair and take her in his arms and place a kiss upon her lips. *What madness is this?* he thought. *Have I taken too much sherry and now my reason is taken from me?*

Just then the telephone on his desk began to ring. Before he could pick up the receiver, Mrs Briggs bid him goodnight and he bid her the same. As he talked to the person who had called him, his mind was on the slim elegant lady that was climbing the stairs and over the voice in his ear, he could hear the stairs creaking as she made her way up to her bed.

# Chapter 5

Oswald was in his favourite chair next to the fire, as usual. He wasn't sleeping, just catnapping and keeping half an eye on the clock. He had decided to venture into the Cathedral in the early hours of the morning, just as he had done a few nights ago, and look for the blue glow in the North Transept again.

As soon as the clock on the mantelpiece rang out one o'clock, Oswald made his way to his secret entrance and into the Cathedral. It was a dark night as the waxing moon was obscured by thick clouds, remnants of the day's earlier rain. Like anvils, they lurched across the sky, black, thick and heavy. It wasn't raining, much to Oswald's relief and he made his way into the Cathedral in quick time.

After passing through his secret entrance and with his eyes adjusted to the dark, he made his way along through the Lady Chapel and on to the South Transept. He passed the effigy of Robert Curthose, eldest son of William the Conqueror, who was buried in the main choir below the great East window and made a right turn through a stone arch. In the dark, Oswald could clearly make out the great brass lectern in the shape of a huge eagle spreading its wings.

He trotted across the tiled floor in front of the great East window. It looked plain and dull with all of its figures and colours obscured by the darkness outside. Right next to the large ornately carved chair, where the Mayor of Gloucester City sat, during important services, there was the other stone archway that led to the North Transept in front of him. Creeping along, slowly and quietly through the archway, Oswald slid himself back below the riser of the stone step he had hidden behind the other night.

Slowly, just as he had done before, he raised his head above the step and peered over it. Everything was as it should be. There was no eerie blue glow anywhere to be seen and Oswald felt an unwelcome feeling of disappointment come over him. He decided that he would explore things further and made his way towards the base of the marble tomb of King Edward II.

He approached the tomb with all the stealth he could manage. Creeping along on his belly, the stone floor beneath him was cold and rough. Edging closer he looked all around himself, nothing was going to surprise him this time. Closer still and always looking about him, he crept towards the tomb. All around there was darkness and an empty brooding silence.

He was in touching distance of the base of the tomb, Oswald could almost feel the cold smoothness of the Purbeck marble. He slithered himself along and craned his neck until it was nearly creaking to see round the first corner. Nothing was out of the ordinary. He pressed the whole of his body almost flat against the wall of the tomb's base and made slowly for the next corner. He peered around the corner, very gingerly and quivering with anticipation. He could feel the fur on the back of his neck beginning to stand on end.

"Hello, Oswald!" at the sound of this voice, Oswald jumped about two feet into the air and came to land on all four of his feet with all his fur standing on end, looking as if he had electrocuted himself. With his teeth chattering together, he looked up to where he had heard the voice come from.

It was his friend, Gideon the mouse. He was looking over the edge of where the effigy of the king was. He was peering down at Oswald with a beaming smile. "What are you doing here?" he asked.

"Wha'…what am *I* doing here? It's me who should be asking *you* that. Haven't you a service to conduct high up in the rafters of the South transept roof," said Oswald, between panting breaths.

"If you are looking for the king, he isn't here. He's taking the night air in the cloister garden, but will return presently. Come on up."

Oswald looked at the height of the tomb where Gideon was and when he had measured the distance accurately with his eyes, with a wiggle of his hindquarters, he leapt up and landed next to his friend. "That was a cheap trick you played on me Gideon, I thought we were friends," said Oswald curtly.

"We are old fruit," replied his friend. "I just couldn't resist it, watching you crawl your way over here. You looked like a snake under a fur rug as you slithered across the floor there." Gideon was laughing at his friend's expense and Oswald felt annoyed and said as much.

"Come, come, you worry too much old chap. So, why *are* you here?"

Oswald explained to his friend that he wanted to seek the blue glow and to find out what it was for himself. "Well," said Gideon. "The blue glow is the ghost of King Edward II who lies buried below this very tomb. As I told you earlier, he usually walks abroad at this time of year during the waxing moon."

Oswald didn't know exactly what to make of that statement and sat and pondered it for a while. *I didn't know ghosts were real,* he thought to himself. Gideon noticed the confused look on Oswald's face and said, "I have been seeing his ghost ever since I was a curate here at the Cathedral. He only walks abroad during the nights of September, you know."

"Is that right?" replied Oswald cynically. "I never thought for one moment that ghosts are real. Have you ever spoken to him?"

"Yes of course I have," replied Gideon. "I have often had conversations with him." Oswald peered round one of the pillars in the direction of the cloister doors to see if the ghost was returning, but there was no sight of the spectre nor its eerie blue glow.

"Why do you think he walks about?" queried Oswald.

"I haven't the faintest idea, old chum. But sometimes, when I am deep in prayer at the high altar in the small hours of the night, I hear the sound of tears being wept."

"And you think it's the ghost," said Oswald.

"Well, it's not the Bishop or the Dean, is it?" replied Gideon, being sarcastic. "Of course it's the king's ghost. I think he's got a very sad story to tell," Gideon added with sympathy.

"So why don't you ask him?" said Oswald.

"Maybe I will, one day," Gideon said at length, washing his ears with his paws.

"Well, I'm off to bed old friend. I must be up early for Matins."

Just before Gideon turned to leave, Oswald remarked "That isn't much sleep!"

"As I get older, I sleep less and less I find. Well, goodnight, old chum."

Oswald watched Gideon scurry down the ornate pillars of the monument they had been sitting on and as he watched his friend disappear around a corner out of sight, he replied "Goodnight, sleep well."

*I think he knows a lot more than he's telling,* thought Oswald. *I wonder why he won't tell me?*

Great Peter, high up in the tower of the Cathedral, chimed out the hours of two o'clock. The sound resonated all around the Cathedral and around the Cathedral close. Oswald was unsure as to whether to stay put and see the ghost for himself alone, or to make his way to the deanery and his warm comfy chair. The decision was taken out of his hands as suddenly the blue glow appeared casting eerie shadows in the dark. His first instinct was to run, but something was making him stay.

Maybe, it was his natural feline curiosity that made him stay put and watch the blue glow getting brighter and brighter as the ghost made its way towards him. As he listened, Oswald could hear the sound of tears being shed. The sound of the sobbing got louder as the glow approached. Oswald could feel the beat of his heart quickening and the fur on his back beginning to stand on edge. If he was going to run, now was the time.

But he didn't! He stayed put and just as the blue glow was right in front of him and it was all that he could see, the glow dimmed in brightness and the figure of a man began to reveal itself. He was tall and broad-shouldered. His face was handsome with a curly beard at the base of his broad chin. The ghost was dressed in a long tunic to his knees and his legs were covered by a thick hose. He wore pointed shoes and beneath the sleeveless tunic, he wore an undershirt. Over all of this, he wore a cloak fastened at the right shoulder.

The face of the man smiled at Oswald and he spoke. "Well," exclaimed the ghost. "If it isn't that little cat again. Hello, fine fellow, fancy seeing you here again." His voice was soft and meaningful and not at all how Oswald had imagined. He spoke slowly and formed his words as if he thought about each one before he spoke it.

"What are you doing here?"

"I'm Oswald!" he replied with deep meaning. "I am the Dean of Gloucester Cathedral's cat."

The ghost looked down at Oswald kindly and smiled and held out his hand to stroke his head.

Oswald didn't flinch, as if he knew what the ghost was going to do before it did it. The large left hand of the ghost cupped the top of Oswald's head and stroked him gently. "It's good to meet you, Oswald. I am Sir Edward of Carnarvon, once King of England and I am most pleased to make your acquaintance."

# Chapter 6

The clouds had eventually cleared and the night sky became studded with stars. The moon, now in her early stages of waxing, could be seen through the stained glass windows of the Cathedral. Streaks of silver light were cutting through the darkness and pools of multi-coloured moonlight were forming on the flagstone floor.

Oswald and the ghost of the king continued their conversation and all the while the ghost continued to stroke Oswald's head. Oswald was loving it and was purring loudly, much to the delight of the ghost.

"I sing in the choir, Your Majesty," said Oswald thorough his purring. "Every service, morning, noon and Evensong."

"Yes," replied the ghost. "I have heard you. You are a very good singer. I would have liked you to sing at my court or at one of my banquets. Queen Isabella, my wife, would have loved your voice." Oswald very much liked the idea of singing at the Royal Court or at a banquet.

Oswald and the ghost talked at length until the early purple streaks of the light of dawn began to creep their way through the panes of coloured glass in the Great East Window. They talked of anything and everything and they enjoyed each other's company.

"I have to go!" announced the ghost. "I will return tonight when the darkness of night has come."

Oswald was disappointed. He very much wanted their conversation to continue.

"I will be here to meet you, your Majesty," he said reluctantly and bowing his head in respect. The ghost leaned forward and stroked Oswald's head again. The hand was large with strong thick fingers and yet, were gentle and caring.

"You don't need to call me 'Your Majesty', Oswald," said the ghost.

"Why not?" replied Oswald, looking confused. "Were you not king?" As he looked up, Oswald could see tears forming in the eyes of the ghost. The expression on its face had changed from happiness to grief. Grief, that Oswald could see hurt very deeply indeed.

"I had my crown taken from me, Oswald. My staff of office was snapped in two in front of me as I lay a prisoner in Kenilworth Castle in 1327." "What happened?" came Oswald's surprised answer.

"What happened?" came Oswald's surprised answer.

"It's a long story, my little friend. The light of the dawn grows ever stronger and I must away," said the ghost looking up at the Great East Window. "We will talk of this tomorrow."

The ghost had gone. Oswald was alone in the silence that surrounded him. Great Peter, struck the hour of five o'clock and he knew that Matins was at eight. He made his way back to the deanery and onto his favourite chair. The embers in the fire had died to a carpet of grey ash and were stone cold. There was an Autumnal chill in the air and Oswald snuggled himself into a tight ball and covered his eyes with his tail.

Sleep was denied him. Until the hour of seven o'clock, Oswald catnapped and his mind went over and over the conversation he had with the ghost. If he *had* slept, he probably would have awakened thinking it had all been a dream. But it had all been real enough and he looked forward to seeing the ghost again that night.

He made up his mind that he would call his friend Gideon down from his chapel in the rafters of the South Transept roof and tell him everything that had happened the previous night. But now it was time for breakfast and Oswald could smell hot buttered kippers.

In the breakfast room of the deanery, the sun was shining through the curtain lace and shadows washed the walls. The Dean was sat in his usual place and was reading the morning paper. The smell of hot kippers and coffee filled the room and

Oswald made his way to the kitchen, where he knew *his* breakfast would be waiting for him.

"Och! There ye are, young Oswald," said Mrs Briggs. "I have breakfast far ye," bending almost double, Mrs Briggs placed a plate of mashed kippers onto the kitchen floor, where Oswald devoured it greedily.

"Slow down. Ye'll be givin' yersel' a belly ache eating like that," she warned with a chuckle in her voice. Oswald wasn't listening to her. The taste of buttered kippers was divine and if he was really lucky, Mrs Briggs would now be pouring the top of the milk into his other bowl.

Soon the kippers were gone and Oswald licked the melted butter off the plate they had been served to him on. Sure enough, next came the top of the milk and then it was time for Matins. Oswald got changed quickly into his red and white choir vestments and made his way into the Cathedral's main quire to take his place.

As usual, Christopher was there and as the organ piped up, the whole choir raised their voices in perfect harmony. Bishop Harriet was conducting the service this morning and there was a good attendance. Oswald especially liked it when Bishop Harriet was taking the service. He felt it added a certain quality to the service.

Bishop Harriet, stood in front of the congregation in all her finery. She wore a white rochet that reached almost to the floor, with a purple Chimere that was finely embroidered with gold. The Mitre she wore also was trimmed with gold and was studded with small coloured jewels. In her left hand, she held her Crozier and with her right hand she made the sign of the cross.

She was a tall lady and some of the clergy at the Cathedral had to look slightly up to meet her gaze. Her shadow was long on the flagstones as the sun streamed through the uppermost windows of the nave. The beams of light were highlighted by the incense that had been burning and some of the congregation likened them to the fingers of God himself.

With Matins soon over, Oswald made it his goal to seek out Gideon and tell him all about the previous night's adventure he had with the ghost and he wanted to tell his friend what had passed between them in conversation. As soon as he had changed out of his vestments, he made his way to the South Transept and up the stairs towards where he knew Gideon would be.

The steps went up in a spiral and were cold and slightly worn in places. Little pieces of some of them were missing and the walls were covered in graffiti both ancient and new. It seemed to Oswald that people liked to let future generations know that they were there at the Cathedral, even if all they were was a name hastily scratched into a wall. Every time he ascended these stairs, Oswald always thought about how many people had climbed them before him over the five hundred and fifty years they had been there.

Up and up and round and round he went until he came to the doorway that led to the roof space above. Here, the stairs were newer and made of wood. As he put his front paw on the first step, he listened carefully. As his ears twitched, he could hear the quiet sound of an organ playing and the throng of very tiny voices singing an old hymn. *Just like Gideon*, thought Oswald. *He always did like the older hymns and always conducting the service in Latin.*

Before he climbed any further, Oswald pondered as to why the mouse Vicar always conducted his services in Latin. It seemed to be a very antiquated way to do things. *Maybe he's just a bluff old traditionalist,* he thought. He climbed the stairs and when he reached the top, he was surrounded by all the mice that had attended Gideon's service. They swarmed round him, all shouting their hellos and waving.

*What it is to be popular,* thought Oswald. He bid each and every one of them a good morning and said how lovely it was to see them all. He didn't venture often to the roof of the South Transept, but when he did, the mice made him most welcome.

When all the hellos had been said and the mice went about their daily business, Oswald walked up to the altar where his friend Gideon was snuffing out the candles. The candles were tall compared to Gideon. They were also thin, like the ones seen on a birthday cake. The smoke from the snuffed candles snaked its way into the air, rolling and tumbling over itself. Gideon had his head bowed in prayer and Oswald waited until he had finished.

At length and without turning round Gideon said "So, you saw and talked with the ghost last night?"

"How could you possibly know that?" Oswald replied a little annoyed that his friend had probably been eavesdropping on them.

"I told you, my friend, that a great many things go on in this place and not much gets past me. What did you talk of?"

Oswald wasn't sure he wanted to continue the conversation in case his friend already knew what had passed between him and the ghost. "We introduced ourselves and we talked about the beauty of the Cathedral and anything and everything else really."

"Mmmm," said Gideon. "Did he tell you his story?"

"No, not yet, we ran out of time. Though he seems keen to do so. We are meeting again tonight and he's going to tell me all."

"Be there as soon after dark as you can be, my friend. There is much to tell," said Gideon.

"Really? How would you know?"

Gideon turned round and peered over the rim of his spectacles, as he always did when he wanted to appear knowledgeable. "Believe me, I know."

Oswald was agitated by his friend's nonchalance and asked the mouse again as to how he knew all that he knew. "When you see the king's ghost tonight Oswald, old friend, everything will be revealed to you and you will see how you will have made a difference to things."

"I just think you are in a peculiar mood," said Oswald annoyed that he had gotten nothing out of Gideon to make things any clearer. "What are you up to for the rest of the day?"

Gideon smiled and said, "I was thinking of taking a stroll around the crypt, I haven't been down there for a while and I would like to see it. Are you thinking of accompanying me?"

"Yes, if that's okay with you?"

"Of course it is. And I will be glad to have your company," Gideon replied.

They made their way down the stairs back into the south transept and headed for the steps that lead down to the crypt. It was one of Gideon's favourite places in the Cathedral as it was very quiet and he could do some really deep thinking down there undisturbed. How much thinking he was going to get done with Oswald for company was a different matter, but he was glad his friend was with him all the same.

# Chapter 7

Meanwhile, back at the deanery, the Dean was sitting in the drawing-room drinking a cup of coffee and reading the morning paper. The day of the concert had arrived and he was looking forward to the event very much. He also hoped that his guest, Mrs Briggs, was looking forward to it as much as he was.

Just as he was turning the page, Mrs Briggs popped her head around the corner of the drawing-room door. "Dean, 'am jis on ma way to the butcher in Northgate Street to fetch some meat fae tonight's dinner. I'll no be lang."

"There's no need, Mrs Briggs!" exclaimed the Dean. "We are dining out tonight and going to the concert."

Mrs Briggs looked surprised and said, "Och! Is it Saturday already? Michty me, how fast the week goes by."

"You hadn't forgotten had you, Mrs Briggs?" enquired the Dean, trying desperately not to sound disappointed.

"No Dean, of course not. However, I will be awa' tae the butcher anyhoo, fae sausages fae a nice Toad in tha' hole fae dinner taemorry."

As soon as she had appeared, Mrs Briggs disappeared and was away to the butcher's shop in the city. Once she had a mind to do something there was no stopping her.

The Dean went back to his newspaper and his coffee and when he was finished with both, he went for a stroll around the garden at the back of the house. He went through the back door and as he did so, he looked at the cat flap and wondered where Oswald might be.

The garden of the deanery had a long sweeping lawn and was immaculately kept by the gardener, Mr Porter. The borders on either side were full of Autumnal colours with

Chrysanthemums, Dahlias and Nerines. It was a huge show of colour for so late in the year. The fountain in the middle of the lawn was switched on and water was tumbling into the basin making the sound of summer rain.

High above him, the sky was clear without a single cloud and the day was warm and tranquil. He decided to return to the house and fetch the novel he was reading. He made himself a glass of lemonade and headed for the steamer chair that was at the bottom of the garden near the green house and Mr Porters' shed.

As he stretched himself out on the steamer chair and began to read, a blackbird was singing in one of the many fruit trees that stood in the borders that edged the lawn on all sides. Their branches were heavy and weighted down with pears, apples, plums and walnuts. *Mrs Briggs will soon be making a lot of use of this harvest,* he thought. With the pleasant thoughts of apple crumble and plum charlotte occupying his mind, he was soon sound asleep and was making slow deep breaths.

It wasn't long before Mrs Briggs returned from the butchers and was putting the sausages she had bought into the fridge. She peered round the door of the Dean's study, only to be disappointed to find it empty. After giving some thought to the whereabouts of the Dean, she entered the drawing room and became most intrigued to find that room too was empty. *Michty me,* she thought. *Where on earth could the Dean be?* Mrs Briggs wandered her way into the dining room and from the dining room into the conservatory. Peering out into the garden she could see the Dean fast asleep on his steamer chair and she decided not to disturb him, for a while at least.

Over the roofs of the houses in Millers Green, Great Peter struck the hour of one o'clock. Mrs Briggs woke the Dean gently, with a tray of egg mayonnaise sandwiches and a pot of hot tea for his lunch. There were rather a lot of sandwiches and on closer inspection, he could see more than one cup and saucer and tea plates. "I thought ye might like some lunch, Dean. Though I am sorry tae waken ye," said Mrs Briggs, tentatively.

The Dean was very pleased to see her and the extra crockery on the tray and he invited her to join him for lunch. Mrs Briggs was pleased to be invited and the two of them ate their lunch in each other's company.

It was like the scene from a watercolour painting. The sun-drenched lawn, the sparkling fountain and the red blush fruit in the trees as the two of them passed the time of day talking and eating, drinking tea and laughing. Several pots of tea and slices of homemade cherry cake. Later, Great Peter chimed five o'clock and Mrs Briggs announced it was time for her to get ready to go out. She parcelled up the tray with the plates and cups and made her way to the kitchen.

The Dean followed suit and made his way to his bedroom, where he, after he had washed, would change his clothes. He opened the doors of the huge oak wardrobe in front of him and looked at all the carefully arranged clothes in front of him. He decided to wear a Linen suit with a white shirt and a navy blue cravat. He had an all leather brown pair of Oxford Brogues that would go with the suit and he laid it all out neatly on the bed before taking a bath.

Once he was dressed, the Dean looked at himself in the full-length mirror he had on the back of the bedroom door. His suit was crisp and clean with seams running down the legs of his trousers that were sharp like a knife blade. He always took pride in his appearance and this evening was no exception. He decided to wait for Mrs Briggs in the hall and he took his place near to the bottom of the stairs.

He didn't have long to wait. Mrs Briggs appeared at the top of the stairs and looked down at the Dean. She was dressed in a summery sky blue dress that finished just above knees and had swirling patterns of deeper blue all over it. On her feet were a pair of white leather open-toed sandals and her legs were bare. Her hair was loose around her shoulders and was a beautiful ash blonde. Mrs Briggs was a picture of loveliness and the Dean felt himself staring at her. "Is something amiss, Dean?" she asked, tentatively.

"No, Mrs Briggs, nothing is wrong, in fact, quite the contrary. You look very beautiful indeed."

"Och Dean, ye'll have me blushin' like a bride with compliments sich as that." Mrs Briggs descended the stairs with a motion that, to the Dean, looked like an angel floating on a cloud. He opened the front door and held out his arm for Mrs Briggs to hold on to and the two of them walked off towards the inn in Westgate Street.

Oswald and Gideon had finished their walk around the crypt and they parted to go their separate ways. Gideon headed to the rafters above the South Transept and Oswald made his way back to the deanery and his supper.

As he went through his flap in the back door of the deanery, Oswald thought it was odd that he couldn't smell anything cooking for dinner. *Drat,* he thought. *I bet it's salad for dinner.* Oswald hated it when salad was on the menu for dinner at the deanery, simply because he would end up with a bowlful of tinned cat meat, his least favourite meal of all.

He wended his way along the hall way and peered round the door of the Dean's study, fully expecting to see the Dean hard at work. To his amazement, the room was empty. *Oh no,* thought Oswald, feeling a wave of dread coming over him. *It's not salad for dinner, there's no dinner at all.* He trotted back to the kitchen and over to the corner where his bowl was. *Yuk*, he thought. *I'm not eating that.* On hearing Great Peter chime five-thirty, Oswald darted out of his cat flap, across Millers Green and back into the Cathedral cloisters. He took a sharp right turn and headed for the monk's kitchen, where he knew he would find Mrs Blake shutting up shop for the night.

Mrs Blake looked up from what she was doing and upon seeing Oswald in front of her she said, "My, my. Look who it is. I go for days not seeing you and now you turn up late for your dinner. Well, let's see what I have for you." Mrs Blake walked over to the big fridges and took out a plate of roasted chicken. She placed it on the floor in front of Oswald and watched with a smile on her face as he made short work of it.

Oswald showed Mrs Blake his gratitude by rubbing round her legs in circles and purring very loudly.

"Now that's enough of that Oswald. It's time for Evensong so go and get changed and be off with you. I will see you tomorrow."

# Chapter 8

The Dean and his housekeeper Mrs Briggs were enjoying their meal in the King William Inn. They were sat at a table with a window that looked over the courtyard garden. All over the courtyard were tables with parasols and chairs with people sat on them eating and drinking. Some were couples, others were families with their dogs. Pots and tubs of flowers were everywhere and in the centre of the courtyard was a large fountain that had a water bearer statue in the middle and water was cascading out from the jug the statue held in its hand.

Looking over the top of his menu, the Dean asked Mrs Briggs, "What will you be having for dessert do you think, Mrs Briggs?"

"I have nae a clue, there's so many to choose from," she replied.

"May I be so bold as to make the suggestion of choosing the Sherry Trifle, Mrs Briggs? It won't be able to hold a candle to yours of course, but it really is quite pleasing all the same.

"Very well. Sherry Trifle it is."

The pair of them engaged in further small talk as they waited for the waitress to come and take their dessert orders.

With their desserts eaten and the bill paid by the Dean, they made their way back to the cathedral for the concert. Evensong had been held in the Lady Chapel and was long over. The nave was filling up with people and when all were seated, a procession made its way from the West Door. Led by Bishop Harriet, the procession included the Mayor of Gloucester and her husband, many members of the City Council and Chapter and other important people from the Cathedral and the City.

"Should ye no be in that procession, Dean?" Mrs Briggs asked.

"Well, in ordinary circumstances, Mrs Briggs, I would be, but I asked Bishop Harriet for the evening off, so that I might be able to bring you to the concert."

"Och ye need not have done that," she replied with a tone of embarrassment and a rosy blush in her cheeks.

"For you, Mrs Briggs, nothing is too much trouble."

All the lights in the nave were dimmed except those that focussed on the stage situated at the foot of the huge main organ. Bishop Harriet stood on the stage and began the evening's entertainment with a short speech, after which everybody applauded loudly. The orchestra began to play and the whole of the Cathedral was filled with the music of Ralph Vaughan Williams.

Back at the deanery, Oswald was curled up in his favourite chair. He had no idea as to where the Dean and Mrs Briggs might be, or what time he would expect to see them home. What he had decided upon was that he was going to cold shoulder them both for leaving him without a decent dinner, despite being served with tinned cat food in his own bowl in the deanery kitchen and Mrs Blake serving him roast chicken. It was the principle of the matter thought Oswald, trying to justify his feelings. He bedded himself down covering his eyes with his front paws and he catnapped the evening away.

The orchestra had decided to do a final encore by playing The Lark Ascending and it received rapturous applause from the audience. Some were so moved by the music that they were making a standing ovation, Mrs Briggs, included. In order that she wouldn't stand out too much, the Dean stood up next to her and applauded the orchestra as enthusiastically as Mrs Briggs.

When all the applause had died away, Mrs Briggs looked the Dean straight in the eyes and thanked him for such a wonderful evening.

"Och Dean, this has been wonderful, thank you so much fae invitin' me."

"Not at all, Mrs Briggs, indeed the pleasure has been all mine. Shall we make our way to the exit, do you think?"

As Mrs Briggs placed her arm into the Dean's they walked slowly towards the south door and out into the night. High above them, the waxing harvest moon was bigger and yellow. The night was very warm and still and as they walked back to the deanery, still arm in arm, Mrs Briggs and the Dean talked and talked.

"I dinna want this night tae end, Dean, I have had such a wonderful time."

"I feel the same way, Mrs Briggs," he replied as he wracked his brain to find somewhere else they could walk to instead of home.

"I wonder if I might tempt you to a walk around Bishop Hooper's monument, Mrs Briggs? My legs are a little stiff from sitting so long on those chairs. Would you care to indulge me?"

"I should like that very much indeed, Dean."

They made their way past the entrance to Millers Green and through St. Mary's Arch, where in front of them was the monument to Bishop Hooper who had died in the sixteenth century for refusing to revert back to Catholicism during the reign of Queen Mary.

The monument was lit up against the night sky by flood lamps and as they walked around its base, the Dean told Mrs Briggs all about the late Bishop. Mrs Briggs was fascinated by the Dean's knowledge and listened intently as they sat on a public bench opposite the monument.

They sat next to each other and turned in slightly so that they could see each other better. They tired the moon with their conversation until at last Great Peter rang out the hour of eleven o'clock.

"Goodness is that the time?" asked the Dean.

Without needing to, Mrs Briggs looked at her watch and replied "Aye, it's eleven o'clock, Dean."

"Mrs Briggs, I wonder if it wouldn't be impertinent of me to ask you to call me by my first name?"

"Goodness Dean, I couldn't possibly do that!" she exclaimed.

The Dean felt a feeling of great disappointment come over him and it must have shown in his face for Mrs Briggs then added, "I have nae idea what it is."

"I see," replied the Dean, laughing at his own naivety. "It's Mark, Mrs Briggs."

"Well," she replied. "I shall only call ye Mark if ye'll call me Caroline."

"It will give me the greatest pleasure, Caroline." He then stood up and held out his hand. "Allow me to walk you home, Caroline, the evening is late and you must be tired."

Mrs Briggs was about to reply in the negative. She didn't want this magical evening to end and if the Dean had requested her to stay out all night, she would have accepted without hesitation. But, being a sensible lady, she took the hand the Dean was offering and rose herself off the bench they had been sitting on and they made their way towards the deanery hand in hand.

With their evening finishing, Oswald's was just beginning. Just as the front door to the deanery opened and the figures of Mrs Briggs and the Dean appeared, Oswald headed out through his flap in the back door.

"I wonder where Oswald is off to so late," said the Dean.

"Och pay him nae mind, Dean, he'll be back afore his breakfast is served tae him," replied Mrs Briggs with a chuckle. "Cats are always oot an' aboot at night."

"Yes," replied the Dean. "They are most certainly."

He turned and looked Mrs Briggs in the eyes. They were deep and blue as the ocean.

*Here were eyes I would be glad to drown in*, he thought.

"Well, I'll away tae ma bed I suppose. I have tae be up early," said Mrs Briggs.

"Oh yes indeed," replied the Dean. "Me too. It's been a long day, but a most enjoyable evening, made all the more lovelier with your presence."

The promise of a kiss was hanging in the air and the Dean wanted to lean forward and kiss his housekeeper on the lips to bid her sweet dreams. But the courage of his conviction was lacking and he chose to take her by the hand instead and as he did so, he placed a gentle kiss upon the back. Mrs Briggs blushed and said, "Och Dean, you are sich a sweet man."

"Not as sweet as you, Mrs Briggs, I'll wager."

Mrs Briggs' rosy cheeks reddened even more at the compliment the Dean had just paid her and she shied away and began heading up the stairs to bed. The Dean stopped her by saying, "Mrs Briggs."

Mrs Briggs stopped climbing the stairs, turned round and came back down to stand in front of him once more. As she looked into his eyes, she could see there was something bothering him and was about to ask him when he said, "I wondered if I might enquire as to what time breakfast will be served," he stuttered.

Looking perplexed, Mrs Briggs replied, "Why Dean, there will be nae breakfast at all, unless…" her words tailed off as if to tease the Dean a little.

"Unless what, Mrs Briggs?"

"Unless you continue to call me Caroline and…"

The Dean could now sense something was going to be said that was to make the whole of the night, so far, seem insignificant.

"And, Mrs, ummm, Caroline?" he corrected himself quickly and he could feel beads of sweat tingling on the back of his neck.

"And ye have tae kiss me properly, Mark. Like a gentleman should kiss his lady. If I am tae be yer lady, that is," she replied.

The Dean moved closer and put his arms around her and drew her nearer to him. As he did so, he tilted his head to one side and before he knew it, their lips met in a passionate kiss. Everything around them seemed to melt away and for the short time the kiss lasted, it was as if they were the only two that existed in the universe.

When their lips parted, Mrs Briggs said, "Goodnight, Mark. Thank you for sich a wonderful evening. I cannae recall when last I enjoyed mysel' so much."

"The pleasure is all mine Caroline and maybe we can do this again sometime, soon perhaps?"

Mrs Briggs replied by saying, "I should like that, Mark. I should like that very much indeed. Goodnight."

As he watched her climb the stairs to her bed, the Dean called out "Goodnight Caroline, sweet dreams."

The Dean headed into the drawing room and poured himself a glass of whisky. He didn't realise that he was shaking until the stopper of the decanter rattled and tinkled back into its place. *Good grief*, he thought to himself. *I'm as giddy as a school boy.* He placed himself into his favourite chair and savoured the rich caramel flavours of the single malt he was drinking.

As the clocks in the deanery all struck the hour of midnight, the Dean rose out of his chair and made his way up to his bedroom. He undressed and put on his pyjamas and pulled back the covers. There was now an Autumnal nip in the air and the Dean was glad he had taken a measure of whisky. He laid down and his head sank into his pillows. Sleep came quickly and soon he was dreaming of where next he could take his housekeeper, now his lady, for a day out together.

# Chapter 9

Oswald, in the meantime, was heading for his secret entrance to the Cathedral. He slipped in past the railings much easier, thanks to limiting himself to just one dinner a day. He trotted through the South Transept and across the main quire until he was sat looking at the tomb of King Edward II once more.

Oswald could never really get used to the deep silence that surrounded him, whenever he was in the Cathedral alone. He was used to hearing music and singing. There was something deep and meaningful about the silence that now surrounded him. With his eyes fully accustomed to the dark, Oswald could make out every detail of the magnificent monument in front of him.

The eerie blue glow was coming up from behind him and was beginning to highlight Oswald's surroundings, making it even easier for him to see. This time he wasn't afraid at all, in fact, he felt relieved that the glow was approaching, because he had been looking forward to seeing the ghost again all day.

"Hello, Oswald," said the ghost.

"Hello, your majesty," Oswald replied, bowing his head. He wished to appear as respectful as possible as he was in the company of royalty.

"It's nice to see you again! How are you?" asked the ghost.

"Oh, very well indeed, your majesty. And how are you?"

"I have much to tell you, Oswald! I want my story, my *true* story to be known to all and I would like you to see that it becomes as widespread as possible. Will you do this for your king, Oswald?"

Oswald was perplexed by what the ghost had said and just as he was going to ask the ghost to clarify what he meant, the ghost said, "Make yourself comfortable. It is gone eleven of the clock and the night will wane away fast."

For the rest of the hours leading up to two o'clock, the ghost told Oswald all about his life. Where and when he was born, what his childhood had been like and what it was like to grow up a prince of the realm. It was a wonderful story and Oswald enjoyed listening to the king's ghost as he told him everything that had happened in his life up to his coronation and crowning.

It was from here on that the ghost's story took on a darker note. The king wasn't so animated in the telling of the story any more, in fact, he had become quite melancholy. He told how his best friend in the whole world, a young man called Piers Gaveston, had been taken from him and was beheaded by the Earls and Barons who despised him. Edward told Oswald how the Barons plotted against him and that they looked down their noses at him because he enjoyed rowing, swimming, digging drainage ditches and thatching roofs. The Barons considered all these things beneath a king's interest and did as much as they could to discourage them.

Edward told how Queen Isabella, his beloved wife, was turned against him by a rich and powerful man called Roger Mortimer, when Edward had met Hugh de Spenser, a young man who he had loved as a brother.

"It was in the year 1327 when my darling Isabella left me and made her way back to her home of France, taking my son. My enemies told me that Mortimer had become her lover and that Isabella no longer loved me and wished me dead."

Oswald felt his ears tingle and his eyes widened when Edward told him this.

"What did you do?" he asked.

The ghost of the king forced a smile, even though Oswald could plainly see that there were tears glistening on his cheeks.

"I took the only option that was open to me, Oswald. I kept my beloved Hugh de Spenser as near to me as possible. I needed all the friends I could muster as they were few and far between."

It was now that the ghost was truly sobbing. He told the most awful story of how Isabella, under the influence of Roger Mortimer, raised an army in France and invaded England. He said that his beloved friend, Hugh de Spencer had been taken prisoner and sent to Hereford where, in the market square, he suffered a terrible death. The ghost also said how he had been taken prisoner himself and taken to Kenilworth Castle, where he was forced to abdicate the throne and had everything taken off him and it was at this time when his staff of office had been snapped in two in front of him and thus signified the end of his reign as king.

The sobs of the ghost were almost too much for Oswald to bear and he tried to console Edward. But it was to no avail. The sorrow of the ghost was pouring out like a river bursting a dam and nothing could stop its flow.

"I was taken Oswald, to Berkeley Castle. The road from Kenilworth was long so we stayed at Llanthony Priory just south of the city of Gloucester." Although he had never actually been there himself, Oswald had heard this place mentioned many times.

"We stayed just one night and we soon entered the battlements of Berkeley Castle. This, my friend, is where the story takes an interesting turn."

The ghost seemed a bit brighter now. He became more cheerful and started to enjoy telling the story again. Oswald listened with renewed interest.

"How long were you at Berkeley for?" he asked.

"Patience, my little stripy friend, patience. All will be revealed to you in time."

As he said this, the ghost was chuckling to himself. All this time the ghost had been walking about in small circles as he told his story to Oswald. But now, as if his feet were aching, the ghost sat down on the floor next to Oswald and he outstretched a hand and began to stroke his ears. Oswald liked this very much and began to purr loudly. This pleased the ghost and so, with renewed energy, he began again.

"It has been told that I met my end at Berkeley Castle. It has been said that I died horribly at the hands of a man called

Maltravers. There are stories abound that I was most sorely treated and eventually put to death by a red-hot poker. But none of it is true. For my darling Isabella issued me with five pounds a day for my keeping and I lived on it most excellently well, until the night of the escape."

Oswald looked at the ghost all perplexed and said, "If life at Berkeley was so good, why did you want to escape?"

Because I wished to be a free man, Oswald. I could have anything I wanted at Berkeley, anything at all, but, if I wanted to stroll around the grounds, I had to be guarded at all times. And when night fell, the door to my room was locked and wasn't unlocked until the dawn. Do you know what it is like not to be able to walk in freedom, Oswald?"

Oswald thought for a minute or two and then told the ghost how once a year he is stuffed into a small plastic box and taken to a place where a tall man in a white coat would poke and prod him and stick a needle in his neck.

"There's no escaping and I hate it," he said.

At this, the ghost chuckled and said, "Just once a year. You wouldn't like nine months then my friend, for that is how long it lasted for me until I was rescued."

Oswald's ears pricked up at the word rescue and the ghost saw this. "Ah, I see that word interests you greatly."

"Indeed it does, your majesty. I am most eager to learn what happened."

The ghost shifted its body sideways slightly as if making himself more comfortable. He tilted his head upwards and looked at the ornate ceiling high above them both.

"It was on the night of the 27th of September 1327 that a gang of men, loyal to me, came to Berkeley Castle."

"Wow!" exclaimed Oswald.

"That was over six hundred years ago this very night."

"Please tell me what happened."

Again the ghost laughed at Oswald's enthusiasm for the story he was telling.

"Very well then, I shall."

As Oswald sat next to the ghost of King Edward II sitting on the decoratively tiled floor of the East Chancel of

Gloucester Cathedral, like two old friends fishing on the bank of the River Severn, the ghost told the story.

"It was a dark moonless night, Oswald. I was locked in my room with a guard outside. I had no idea he was loyal to me. His name was Hogben. He was a young lad, very tall and broad shouldered like me. As the hour of midnight approached, a gang of men led by a loyal subject of mine called Stephen Dunheved gained entrance to the castle by a secret passage. The men entered my room and they all dropped to their knees in homage to me. I was told to gather my things very quickly and we sped off towards the outer walls of the castle."

"But the guards had seen us and there was a terrible sword fight between us and the men of the castle. We all managed to escape, all of us except Hogben. He suffered a mortal wound to his chest and he died quickly. We sped off into the night and I was hurried towards the coast, where a boat awaited to carry me to France."

"It was here that Stephen Dunheved and his gang of men and I went our separate ways. I was given clothing to disguise myself as a pilgrim and a good deal of money for board and lodgings on my journeys. I was also given a small wooden box and I was told never to let anyone at all see what was inside it and to guard the contents of the box with my very life."

Over the few hours that remained until dawn, the ghost told Oswald that he visited churches and monasteries all over France, eventually meeting the Pope himself at Avignon and that it was during this meeting that arrangements were made for Edward II to meet his son, the young King Edward III.

"What happened to the body of the guard, Hogben?" asked Oswald.

The ghost looked down at him and smiled as he answered.

"From what I have been told, he was taken back to the cell where I was being held. An old wise woman was summoned from the nearby village of Berkeley and was told to prepare the body for burial. As she was left alone in the room to do her duties, she performed an incantation to preserve my soul for all time. She had no idea that I had escaped and that the body she was saying the incantation over was Hogben, my guard as his face was covered at all times. Some two months later Hogben's body was laid to rest here in the Cathedral and this wonderful monument was erected over it."

All the while, Oswald listened with great interest to all that the ghost had to say, until the light of dawn came streaming through the Great East Window. It was now that the ghost had to retire until once again the moon was high in the sky.

"Tomorrow is the full moon Oswald, our last chance to meet until next September. I will finish the story then. Until tonight, my little friend, I bid thee adieu."

To his amazement the shape of the ghost dissipated before Oswald's very eyes. *I wonder how he does that*, he thought.

Suddenly realising that his belly was empty and that Mrs Briggs would soon be serving breakfast at the deanery, Oswald made his way home. It was a bright morning, but a chill wind was blowing and it ruffled Oswald's fur as he walked towards the deanery in Millers Green.

As he approached the deanery, Oswald headed around the back to where his cat flap was in the back door. He slipped himself in and the aroma of bacon being fried met his keen nostrils, as he entered the kitchen. He planned to have a good breakfast and a good sleep on his favourite chair in the drawing room.

# Chapter 10

After a rather speedy breakfast, Oswald got changed and made his way to the main quire in the Cathedral, where Bishop Harriet was performing Matins. The whole choir had gathered and as usual, Christopher was next to Oswald in the choir stalls. He was a little disappointed in that Bishop Harriet had chosen a Te Deum, rather than the Magnificat for the service. However, he put all his heart and soul into his singing.

After Matins, Oswald was free until Evensong and he decided to take it easy for the day so that he would be fresh to meet the ghost one last time after nightfall. Once he was out of his vestments, Oswald made his way back to his favourite chair in the deanery drawing room and it was there that he stayed all day.

It was a warm and sunny late September day and the Dean invited Mrs Briggs to have tea with him in the garden. Gladly, Mrs Briggs accepted and made some scones for the occasion. Sat on a plate of the best china, the scones were fat and round and warm and smelled divine.

Out in the garden there was a blend of warm scones, best butter, homemade strawberry jam and whipped cream. It was like an idyllic afternoon, the sun was warm and the company was convivial.

"Mrs Briggs," began the Dean. "Sorry, Caroline. Your scones are really lovely and your homemade jam is a triumph. If you don't mind me saying so?"

"Why thank you, Mark. It's my Grandmother's recipe fae both ye know. I remember as a wee gal, I used to sit in my Grandmother's kitchen watching her make all kinds of wonderful things tae eat. She handed me her recipe book on ma twenty first birthday. It wis nae long afore I married ma husband."

Not wishing to sound wistful, Mrs Briggs offered another cup of tea and another scone with jam and cream which the Dean accepted readily.

"May I enquire as to how long you both were married?"

"Jis three years. It was an accident at the foundry where he worked as a metal forger. He wis a lovely man, Mark. Very akin tae you in fact," she added more cheerfully.

"I really am sorry for your loss, Caroline. You bear it with great fortitude."

Mrs Briggs sighed and stared into space as she said, "It were a long time ago the now. Twenty-five years in fact. Michty me how time passes. I still think of him, almost every day."

The Dean smiled and placed his hand reassuringly on top of hers and said, "As long as he is remembered, he will never be truly gone."

While the Dean and Mrs Briggs whiled away the afternoon romantically in the garden, Oswald cat napped in his favourite chair. Not moving at all except to rearrange himself. The clock on the mantelpiece chimed away the hours until Evensong.

Evensong on a Sunday was early. Usually the service began at five o'clock, but Sunday was different and began at two o'clock.

Oswald took his usual place next to Christopher in the choir stall. As he looked at Christopher, it seemed that the gap where his front teeth were missing, was widening. He dared himself to take a closer look, but it was no use. As soon as Christopher smiled at him, Oswald began to chuckle uncontrollably. *Calm yourself,* he thought. But he looks so comical, he said to himself, as the organ piped up and voices were raised in song.

His duties for Evensong were finally over, Oswald made his way back to the kitchen at the deanery, where Mrs Briggs was cooking a delightful Toad in the Hole. A perfect marriage of sausages baked in batter. It was served with mashed potatoes and green vegetables and lashings of rich, hot gravy.

His dinner was already in his bowl in its usual corner, when Oswald came through the flap in the back door. Instead of seeing Mrs Briggs sitting on her own eating at the kitchen table, there was no one there to greet him as he came in. So, without much more ado, Oswald ate his dinner of toad in the hole and gravy and sat on the floor washing and waiting for dessert. He could hear Mrs Briggs and the Dean talking and laughing in the dining room and it wasn't long before he was tucking into a bowl of rich creamy custard.

In the dining room, the Dean and Mrs Briggs were eating apple tart and custard and when they had finished their meal, for the very first time, Mrs Briggs allowed the Dean into the kitchen to help her wash the dishes. All the while, they were talking and laughing and the dishes were soon all clean and tidied away.

Oswald was in his usual seat in the drawing room and a good blaze had been set in the grate. Outside it was cold and dark, but inside, it was cosy and warm. He was just drifting off into a peaceful sleep, when the Dean and Mrs Briggs entered into the room. They were carrying cups of coffee and the Dean offered Mrs Briggs a seat, Oswald's seat to be exact.

"Don't mind Oswald, Caroline!" exclaimed the Dean. "He'll go upstairs to sleep on my bed, he doesn't mind at all. Do you, old chap?"

If looks could kill, then the Dean would be quite dead after the stare Oswald had given him for turfing him out of his favourite chair. He left the room wagging his tail in a very annoyed manner and made his way upstairs, to sleep on the Dean's bed, where there was no fire and no cosy atmosphere.

Oswald entered the Dean's bedroom and jumped up onto the bed, where he then turned several circles and laid himself down. Although the bed was comfy, the room was cold. But he was soon as warm as freshly made toast. It was no substitute, however, for a cosy armchair in front of a blazing fire.

Downstairs in the drawing room, the Dean and Mrs Briggs were talking and laughing and enjoying each other's company. They talked of everything and anything and the hours were melting away, as the two of them didn't notice any of the clocks in the deanery striking.

After a glass or two of sherry each, the fire was dying down low and the chill of the evening made Mrs Briggs shiver.

"My dear," said the Dean. "You are cold! Shall I build the fire again?"

"Och no! I will be away to ma bed the now, the hour is late and I must be up early for the market come the morning."

"Well, good night my sweet! Thank you for a lovely evening," said the Dean and he kissed her gently on the lips. "Good night Mark, sleep well."

"I will," replied the Dean. "If you are in my dreams."

Mrs Briggs left the room and climbed the stairs to her bed. As she ascended, the stairs made their usual creaks and squeaks and then the Dean heard her say good night to Oswald as she passed the Dean's bedroom door.

It had been a most enjoyable evening with a superb meal and excellent company all rounded off by a romantic chat in front of the fire. He decided that he would like to make some sort of celebration, in honour of the evening going so well and so he crossed the room to where a crystal decanter and some glasses were standing on a sideboard and poured himself a small glass of whisky.

As he looked at the dying embers of the fire through the amber liquid in his glass, he could almost see the warmth of the whisky glowing. He raised the glass to his nose and wafted it from side to side and breathed in the whisky's rich aromas. He took a sip and savoured the flavours of the whisky before swallowing it slowly.

The whisky was warming and satisfying and brought about the Dean a deep feeling of mellowness and satisfaction. Just as he was about to take a second sip, Oswald came in and looked at the Dean in a scornful manner.

"Now then, Oswald, don't be like that old friend. Mrs Briggs and I are very good friends and we are going to be a lot closer to each other now. Yes, very close indeed. Almost like were we in love..." the Dean's voice tailed off as he entered into deep thought.

*Could it be true; could he be in love with Mrs Briggs? Goodness*, thought the Dean. *I think I am in love with Mrs Briggs, I mean Caroline.* He looked at Oswald, who now was sitting in the chair Mrs Briggs had been sitting in, and said aloud, "Oswald, old friend, I am in love. Do you hear me; I am in love," he exclaimed with a louder voice.

*Keep on like that and you will have your love out of bed and giving you a piece of her mind,* thought Oswald. The Dean finished his whisky and with a stroke of his head as he passed his chair, he bade Oswald good night.

The clock on the mantelpiece was the first to strike the hour of midnight. Oswald lept out of his chair and sped out of the deanery and towards his secret entrance to the Cathedral. He hadn't realised it was so late and he hoped that he hadn't kept the ghost waiting too long. He hadn't time to look up at the full moon who was glowing in a cloudless sky and was lighting the Cathedral gardens with its silvery light.

Once through his secret entrance, he crossed the main quire and as he rounded the corner, he could see the blue glow of the ghost. As he got nearer, he could see the ghost sitting on the steps and looking downwards. The ghost appeared to be talking to something and as he drew nearer, Oswald could see that the ghost was talking with Gideon. "Ah, there you are!" said the ghost as it looked up at Oswald. "I thought you might not be coming my friend."

Through the rapid panting of his breath, Oswald replied "I am most sorry, your majesty, I was enjoying a good dinner and I kind of drifted off to sleep and..."

"It is of no matter," interrupted the ghost. "You are here now and there is much to tell."

Oswald looked down at Gideon and said, "Hello, Gideon. What are you doing here?"

Gideon looked over the rim of his glasses as he usually did if he wanted to look wise and said, "I am here to help tell the last part of the king's story."

"You!" exclaimed Oswald. "How do you fit into all of this?"

Gideon smiled and said "All will be revealed soon. Now sit and listen, there is much to hear."

The ghost smiled and looked at Oswald and said, "Now, my friend, this is where the story ends. After journeying all over France and Germany, dressed as a holy pilgrim, I eventually made my way to Italy.

I came across a monastery called Saint Antonio di Butrio and I asked to see the abbot there, Father Manuel Fieschi. I was given food and allowed to rest until after Vespers. It was then I was invited into the abbot's chamber."

"I introduced myself as Edward of Caernarvon, a simple man on holy pilgrimage. I said I was seeking a place at the Monastery to pray and to find peace and solitude. The Abbott agreed to let me stay and I was given the task of tending the gardens of the

Monastery. I had to give up all my earthly possessions to enter the Monastery and so I had to give the Abbott the wooden box I had guarded so securely. The Abbott assured me that it was in safe hands."

Oswald and Gideon look on as they listened to the story the ghost was relating to them. They were listening intently and hanging on every word the ghost said.

"Do continue, my lord," said Gideon.

"Yes," replied Oswald. "Please go on."

The ghost looked down and smiled at the both and as he stroked Oswald's ears, he continued his story.

"All was well for about two years. I was happy in the Monastery gardens, tending the plants in the yearlong warm sunshine. It was peaceful and I was able to leave the terrible things that had happened to me and my friends behind me."

"Then, one day, a group of three armoured riders came to the Monastery and demanded to see the Abbott. They were shown to his chamber and I could hear raised voices.

Eventually the riders left and I was summoned to the Abbott's chamber. Once I was there, he took the wooden box I had given him and, despite my objections, he opened it. He looked inside the box, his eyes lit up and then he looked at me open mouthed."

"What was in the box?" cried Oswald, very excited. "Jewels, treasure, something good to eat?" he quizzed.

"No," replied the ghost. "It was my ring of office and the royal seal. The marks of a King of England. My true identity was now revealed," the ghost said and he became very saddened.

"Those armoured men came looking for the king," said Gideon to Oswald. "They were searching far and wide all over Europe because rumours of the king's survival were abound. The men had come to the Monastery to convince the Abbott that Edward of Caernarvon was King Edward II of England and that he hadn't died at Berkeley Castle and had escaped and he was to return to England with them."

"Goodness!" exclaimed Oswald. "What convinced the men to leave?"

"Well," replied Gideon, "they were tall men and very strong looking and were very resolute in their purpose. They carried huge swords and their horses were massive and—"

"Wait a minute!" interrupted Oswald. "How do you know all this? You weren't there! Or *were* you?" Oswald thought for a second or two and then said, "You *were*; you were there too. But how? And how come you are still alive now after so many years have passed?"

Gideon looked at his friend and smiled and said, "It's all pretty simple, the armoured men were told to leave and that their suspicions surrounding Lord Edward of Caernarvon were ridiculous. And so, they left, but not before vowing to return. I will tell you more after the king's story is completed. Do continue my lord."

The ghost continued his story by saying, "The Abbott took the ring and royal seal out of the box and looked at me. He then lowered his head in homage and said, 'Your Royal Majesty.'"

"I didn't know what to do and I just stood there for a while gathering my thoughts. At first I thought I should run until the Abbott said that my secret was safe as long as I wanted it to be. It was later in 1337 that I thought the world should know that I had survived my imprisonment at Berkeley castle and that the attempt on my life had failed. I wanted it known that I was alive and well and living at Saint Antonio di Buttrio Monastery, tending the gardens there."

"The Abbott wrote a letter to my son, King Edward III, who had, by now, deposed

Roger Mortimer and had him executed for Treason and had his mother, my wife and Queen, Isabella, retired to her castle home in Norfolk where she died in 1358. After I was deposed and sent to Berkeley Castle, I never saw her again." The ghost began to sob and Oswald looked at Gideon.

The ghost began to sob and Oswald looked at Gideon.

"Where do you fit into all of this?"

"Well," said Gideon smiling. "The incantation, the wise woman from Berkeley village, said over the body of Hogben the guard, instead of the king, to preserve his soul, must have had the same effect on me because I was in the room at the time. I had often been in the room with the king whilst he was kept prisoner there and we knew each other very well."

"As the battle to free the king from Berkeley Castle raged on, I raced down the stairs past all the fighting and jumped into the King's belongings. I stayed in there until we were in France and I popped out whilst the king was resting one afternoon. He was pleased to see me and I him. Then, we travelled together and the years rolled by and I noticed that I wasn't getting any older. The life of a mouse my friend is about three years; after eight years I knew something had happened to me," he concluded.

Gideon looked up at the king who was now more composed and was smiling at him as he told Oswald his story.

"We lived together at Saint Antonio di Bittrio for many years," said the king.

"Once my son had received the Abbott's letter in England, arrangements were made for me to meet him at the Court of Pope Benedict the Twelfth at Avignon. We met in secret and spoke at length of everything. We were together for nine days and then we had to part."

"It was good to see him and talk to him and arrangements were made for me," said the king, with intrigue in his voice. Oswald looked confused at Gideon and Gideon just smiled back with a very knowing look on his face.

Looking at the base of the tomb, Oswald said, "So that isn't you that lies there, my lord?"

"Yes it is," replied Gideon. Looking up at the king, he said, "With your permission my lord."

"With my blessing, dear friend," replied the king.

"You see Oswald, old friend, the king lies in his tomb here," said Gideon.

"Arrangements were made with King Edward III to have his father's bones removed from his tomb at the Monastery of Saint Antonio in Italy and placed here under this monument after Hogben's bones were taken out. It happened in the year 1687 under the reign of King James II. I was here to witness it all."

"I remember the day they came to remove my bones," interrupted the ghost. "I felt the earth moving and felt the spades impact the materials that covered my plain and ordinary coffin. Then my bones were taken and put into a casket that was brightly decorated and my long journey to England began."

"And what about poor Hogben, who had served so well? What happened to his bones?" asked Oswald.

"They were taken and laid to rest in the tomb at Saint Antonio, where he was buried with full honours," replied the king. Looking up at the Great East Window, the faint glimmer of dawn could be seen.

Looking up at the Great East Window, the faint glimmer of dawn could be seen.

"It will soon be time for me to say adieu one last time my friends," he said sadly.

"Must you go?" asked Oswald.

"Indeed I must. The September moon is gone and I must away. You now know my true story Oswald and now I can be at peace for I am content to know my story is known. I will now fade away and rest for all eternity. I need no longer walk the earth. But worry not, for we shall all meet again."

The three of them bade their fond farewells and with a smile and a cheerful wave the ghost began to fade from their sight. Oswald and Gideon lowered their heads in homage to the king and when they looked up, the ghost was gone.

"What do you think he meant when he said we would all meet again?" asked Oswald.

"What he means is that now that *his* spirit rests, *my* time to rest will now follow. I shall no longer live for centuries and I will one day fall asleep and be with the king once more."

Oswald sniffed back a tear. "I shall miss you sorely."

Gideon gave his friend a reassuring smile and said, "You too will join us, when your time comes. Fear not and always remember, we shall all be together forever, very soon, but not yet."

Gideon's words cheered Oswald and he smiled as he said, "I will look forward to it."

"So will I my friend, so will I."

# Chapter 11

Outside, the autumn morning was dry and bright and the sun still had some heat about it. Oswald walked towards the deanery and to where his breakfast would be. He entered the deanery through his flap and looked around the kitchen. There was the usual smells and aromas of sausage and bacon and Oswald licked his lips with delight. He walked into the breakfast room and saw both the Dean and Mrs Briggs enjoying breakfast together.

Oswald walked under the table and brushed against the Dean's leg.

"Ah! There you are you lazy cat. Have you been in bed all this time? Breakfast is nearly over."

The Dean picked up a sausage with his fork and without thinking he dropped it onto the rug in front of Oswald.

"Oh Caroline, I am so sorry, I wasn't thinking."

Mrs Briggs just laughed and said that it was fine and that if Oswald wanted another, he was to have it.

"I'm as dotty aboot that cat as ye are Mark," she chuckled.

Oswald purred loudly as he ate his sausage and as soon as it was gone, down fell another for him to enjoy.

Above him, the Dean and Mrs Briggs were talking and finishing their coffees.

"I do hope you will pardon me this morning my sweet, but I have to go into the city to buy something I need. I will of course help with the dishes first."

"Och, ye'll do nae sich thang," replied Mrs Briggs. "I can do the dishes, ye have much more important thangs tae attend tae."

As the Dean rose out of his seat and left the room, he smiled to himself and thought you couldn't be more right.

Oswald finished his last sausage and climbed into his favourite chair in the drawing room. The clock on the mantelpiece chimed ten and Oswald catnapped the rest of the morning away. There was no service in the Cathedral this morning for Oswald to sing at and so he was free to do as he pleased.

Meanwhile, in the kitchen, Mrs Briggs was about her duties tidying up the breakfast things and washing the dishes. As she hummed to herself, she couldn't help thinking what the Dean had to go into the city for. He usually did his shopping on a Saturday afternoon and she wondered what could have called him away so urgently on a Thursday morning.

Just then, the telephone in the Dean's study rang and Mrs Briggs picked up the receiver.

"Good morning, the deanery the hooskeeper Mrs Briggs speaking."

"Good morning, Mrs Briggs. How are you?"

It was Bishop Harriet calling from the Bishop's palace just down the road.

"Is the Dean there, please?"

"Och no, am sorry yer Grace but Mark, am mean the Dean has just popped oot tae the city. Can I tak a message?"

"No that's fine, Mrs Briggs. I'm seeing him this afternoon at a meeting. I will speak to him then. Good morning, Mrs Briggs."

"Aye an a gid morning tae ye, yer Grace."

Mrs Briggs replaced the receiver of the telephone and went about her duties once more. Time was getting on and soon lunch would be ready and the Dean wasn't back yet. *His meeting with Bishop Harriet was at two o'clock and he mustn't be late,* she thought.

All this time Oswald was catnapping in his chair. The day was beautiful and the sun streaming through the drawing-room windows was both bright and warm. He didn't care a button as to where the Dean might be or that he might be late for his meeting. Oswald was warm and cosy in his chair, his belly was full and that was all that mattered to him.

The clocks in the deanery all struck the hour of one. Then they chimed a quarter past and Mrs Briggs was beginning to worry. The half past chimes were made and just as Mrs Briggs was picking up the telephone to call Bishop Harriet to say the Dean might be late to their meeting, when in burst the Dean through the front door. "Michty me Dean, where have ye been all this time? Bishop Harriet called aboot ten o'clock an I was aboot to call her to say ye might be late to yer meeting."

"Don't trouble yourself with that Caroline, I am here now and I shall make my way to the meeting now. Plenty of time," he exclaimed.

"Ye have nae had any lunch, Mark," she called after him as he disappeared round the front of the pillars of the gate.

"No time for lunch, Caroline. Much more important things are afoot."

"Well now!" said Mrs Briggs.

I wonder why he is actin so strange this morning?" she said to Oswald, who barely flicked an ear.

"Yer nae help, ye daft cat," she said as she made her way back to the kitchen.

*What shall I do with this soup I made fae lunch*? she thought. *I cannae throw it away, that's wasteful. Maybe I can make it into a stew with beef and dumplings. Mark will leek that, I think.*

The Dean arrived back at the deanery just before six o'clock. As he entered through the front door, Mrs Briggs called from the kitchen. "Is that ye Dean?"

The Dean made his usual reply and added, "I hope dinner is ready early Caroline, I'm famished."

"Ah've made a beef stew with dumplings using the soup I had made fae lunch that ye had nae time for."

"I am sorry about that Caroline, but I had something very important to get in the city."

"Well, I hope it was important enough fae ye to skip yer lunch."

"It was," he assured her.

"And neither could I miss the meeting I had with Bishop Harriet. That was equally important."

"Aye, well that's as maybe. I'll serve dinner early, as it's ready on the hob."

"It smells lovely, Caroline. I can't wait."

Mrs Briggs returned to the kitchen and came back carrying a large saucepan filled with beef stew and dumplings. Oswald had been ignoring the delightful aromas coming from the kitchen all afternoon, but once the stew had been served, that was it, he just had to have some. He trotted past the dining room door on his way to the kitchen and as he went, Mrs Briggs called after him "There's stewed beef, gravy and a dumpling in yer bowl fae ye Oswald."

Chocolate sponge with vanilla sauce was the dessert and it was equally enjoyed as the beef stew had been.

"What was so important that ye had tae miss yer lunch today, Mark?"

"Well, Caroline, I'm really glad you asked, because I have something very important to say to you."

Mrs Briggs looked quite startled and wondered what it might be that the Dean was about to impart to her.

Then he got out of his chair and walked over to her. As he did so, he pulled something out of the rear pocket of his trousers.

"I have something for you Caroline. We have been enjoying all these evenings together here at the deanery and at the concert and enjoying walks together and having tea in the garden. I really wouldn't want all this to end."

"I too have enjoyed it, Mark. It has been truly lovely."

"Then, Caroline, I wonder if you would do me the honour of..."

His speech dropped off as he went down on one knee and opened a small blue box that contained a sapphire and diamond ring.

"...Becoming my wife," he continued.

"Bless me!" exclaimed Mrs Briggs. "I dinna know whit tae say."

"Then please say yes," pleaded the Dean.

"Oh, Mark, of course I say yes. How could I say anything else? Yes, my darling, yes I will marry ye."

"Caroline," said the Dean.

"You have made me the happiest man alive today. I met with Bishop Harriet this afternoon to seek her consent and she has agreed and will perform the ceremony should we wish her to."

Mrs Briggs looked at the ring in the box that the Dean was still holding out for her. She took it from the box and placed it on her finger. As the diamonds sparkled in the candle light, she said, "What a beautiful ring."

"It was my mother's," replied the Dean.

"I had it altered for you at the jewellers and I hoped you would like it. She would be pleased for you to have it."

"And I will be honoured to wear it, Mark. Thank you," she said as she leaned forward to kiss him.

Just as their lips met Oswald appeared in the doorway of the dining room. *Hello*, he thought, *what's all this then*? What's he doing down there, dropped something has he?

Then the Dean turned to him and said, "Oswald! Caroline and I are in love and we are going to be married. The three of us shall be together for always, what do you say to that?"

*I'll tell you what I think of that,* thought Oswald. *Where on Earth is my vanilla sauce?* And he let out a loud mew.

"I know what he's wanting," said Mrs Briggs.

"Alright Oswald, I'll get ye yer dessert."

As Mrs Briggs placed the saucer of vanilla sauce in front of him, Oswald let out a loud purr and began to rub himself against her legs.

"Now who's a happy cat?" she asked.

*I am,* thought Oswald.

That evening, the Dean and Mrs Briggs were taking a walk through the Cathedral, Oswald was following them and as they all walked up the steps, they stopped in front of Edward II's tomb. Oswald leapt up and perched himself near the feet of the king's effigy. He looked back at them both as they stood there hand in hand.

Mrs Briggs turned to the Dean and asked, "I wonder if he *is actually* in there?"

"No one knows," replied the Dean and they both started to walk away. Oswald let out a loud mew and they both turned back to look at him.

"Do *you* know if he is in there, Oswald?" asked Mrs Briggs.

"He probably wouldn't tell us, even if he did," laughed the Dean as he walked on.

Mrs Briggs stood there for a little while and said to Oswald, "I think ye do know, don't you?

Oswald looked her straight in the eye and winked and seemed to smile. *Oh yes*, thought Oswald, *I do know. And so do you now, dear reader.*